Mumbo Jumbo's SHOES

Peter Haswell

One morning, Mumbo Jumbo woke up.

He got up . . .

2

took off his pyjamas . . .

and put his clothes on.

Mumbo Jumbo looked out of the window.

'I'll go for a walk,' he said.

'Now, where did I put my shoes?'

Mumbo Jumbo went to his chest of drawers.

He pulled everything out.
But he didn't find his shoes.

Mumbo Jumbo went to his wardrobe.

He pulled everything out.
But he didn't find his shoes.

Mumbo Jumbo went into the kitchen.

He pulled everything out.
But he didn't find his shoes.

Mumbo Jumbo went to the cupboard.

He had pulled almost everything out when . . .

a clock fell on his foot.

'My shoes!' cried Mumbo Jumbo. 'I've found
my shoes. Now I can go for a walk. But . . .

"Where is the front door?"